THE
KINSMAN

HOLLY SHEIDENBERGER

MAHONIA
PUBLISHING

MAHONIA
— PUBLISHING —

For L.A. studio musicians past and present,
whose names are unknown to most,
but who are among the best in the world
and without whom the last century would not have
been possible

Dear Camille...

1

Dear Camille,

Most days make absolutely no difference.

But sometimes a single day can change your entire life forever. Those don't come very often, but when they do, you can only hope that they change things for the better.

Most of the time, they don't.

One day you will understand the truth about your father. I will lie to you today, and every day after, about what really happened. Why? Because I've learned that truth doesn't matter.

Truth doesn't pay your rent, or your legal bills, or your funeral costs.

But someday, when you are old enough to know, I will tell you about your past. By then it may be too late. It will be my word against everybody else's, but even I will have lied to you since you were born.

It will be up to you to decide who you really are. Who you want to be.

Perhaps it's best if I just tell you what happened on the

five fateful days that changed everything.
   The first was one year ago, today.
   I only hope you can forgive me.
   Love,
   Your Mother

The First Day

JANUARY 20

2

My husband was missing for an hour and forty-seven minutes.

To most people, that probably seems like nothing more than a traffic jam and a dead cell phone battery. Either of those was extremely likely, since we lived in Los Angeles. But my Cameron was due home an hour and forty-seven minutes ago, and if I hadn't heard from him, something was wrong.

I paced the floor in our tiny apartment, clutching my phone like it was my lifeline to him. I checked the screen every thirty seconds, as if doing so would force it to ring. The countless voicemail messages and texts I left him elicited no response. Neither did the phone call I made to his brother Jason, with whom he had lunch that afternoon.

Was it too soon to call the police?

I called Cameron again instead. Still no answer.

My voice quavered into his voicemail. "Cam, it's Lara. Please, baby, call me."

The local evening news droned softly in the

background. I'd turned it on half an hour before, just in case there was an accident on the freeway, or anything else that would explain Cameron's failure to come home to me. So far, nothing.

Maybe we'd had a miscommunication about his plans. I thought he was going to be home for dinner, but maybe he intended to have dinner with Jason, as well as lunch. If that was the case, then he wouldn't even turn his phone on until later.

I felt a slight relief at that idea. That was probably it. I was being paranoid. To prove it to myself, I went back over the events of the day in my mind to figure out what I had missed.

The morning started out normal for us. Well, workday-normal anyway. Cameron and I were studio musicians in Los Angeles, and we didn't work every day. We would go in to play our instruments (him trumpet, me piano) for recording sessions whenever we got called for a gig.

That morning, we were both scheduled to play for a television show, so we woke up at the ungodly hour required to sit in traffic long enough to arrive at the studio by nine o'clock. Coffee, breakfast, shower, and more coffee for the road. Workday-normal.

After the session, the studio was buzzing with musicians packing up their instruments and hustling to get back on the freeway before the afternoon traffic got bad. Well, worse anyway. It was always bad.

Above the din and across the room, I spotted Cameron's disheveled red hair. He felt my eyes on him, looked up, and winked. I pushed my bench away from the piano and stood up, probably blushing. He still did that to me.

By the time I made my way over to him, a trombone player was telling him a crazy story about the eighty-year-old neighbor lady strutting around in a leopard-print bikini, trying to seduce the pool guy. Cameron was roaring with laughter.

Cameron slipped his arm around my waist and kissed me on the head. So far, so normal. He grabbed both his trumpet cases and I carried his mute bag. We walked out to the parking garage together. He loaded everything into the trunk of his car, and I slid behind the wheel.

Usually, we'd head straight home and have lunch together, but that day Cameron had planned to have lunch with Jason. He wasn't looking forward to it, but he wouldn't tell me why. He said he'd explain later.

The plan was for me to drop Cameron off at Jason's church, and then I would continue on home. They were going to spend the afternoon together, and I was almost certain Cameron said Jason would drop him by our apartment that night. How could I have gotten that wrong?

I checked my phone again. Still nothing from either Cameron or Jason. Shouldn't at least one of them have been checking their phone?

By then, Cameron was more than two hours late to get home. I started to catastrophize all the possible explanations for why he wasn't there. Most of them were completely implausible, such as him cheating on me or lying to me. Cameron would never do that.

But if he was in an accident…

I couldn't let my mind go there. I was afraid I would break down completely.

For some reason, I started to think about Jason.

Pretty much everyone would agree that what Cameron and I did for a living was unusual. But if our job was weird, Jason's was weirder. He was the Head Pastor of a mega-church in South Central Los Angeles.

A picture of him flashed into my mind. He and Cameron definitely shared a family resemblance, except for their hair color (Jason's was dark), but only if you looked at Jason really closely. He was almost forty, but he took extreme measures to project the image of being eternally twenty-five. He had the youngest, hippest haircut a guy with a gently receding hairline could get away with. He also worked out obsessively, and I was pretty sure Botox was part of his self-care routine.

It was all very high-maintenance and a bit ridiculous. But despite that, Jason was actually a really great guy. Just as charismatic as Cameron, if not more. He was funny, too, and could have Cameron rolling with laughter when they got to trading stories. He and his wife Alexis used to invite us over for dinner every month, and the guys would razz each other mercilessly while Alexis rolled her eyes at me.

The thing that stood out most about Jason was how important family was to him. He constantly sermonized about how we should all get to know each other better, one on one. To strengthen our bond as a family.

As a result, I invited Alexis to meet for coffee a few

times, but she always turned me down. Eventually I stopped asking, figuring she was too busy with all her volunteering at the church.

That didn't stop Jason, though. He called and invited me to go to dinner with him, just the two of us. I knew his intentions were good, but I felt uncomfortable with the idea anyway. I wriggled out of it with some awkward excuse.

When I told Cameron about it later, he was not amused. He muttered something about "No way in hell," said he would tell Jason to back off, and that was the end of that.

Something on the TV caught the attention of my wandering mind. It was a shot from the traffic cam on the 101 freeway. That's the freeway Cameron and Jason would have taken.

My heart shot into my throat.

I tried to swallow it back down.

The newscaster described a fatal accident in the mellowest tone possible, which infuriated me.

Was Cameron involved in the accident? Could it be…?

I peered at the TV screen, trying to see the cars involved, but the image was too fuzzy. I swiped at my forehead, tears springing to the surface.

No, I told myself. No. It wasn't him. It couldn't be.

The newscaster continued on, explaining that one woman died at the scene, and there was only one other person with minor injuries.

I breathed a sigh of relief. It couldn't have been Cameron.

Then where was he?

I checked my phone again.

Dialed his number again.

Voicemail again.

A sick feeling settled into me. It was familiar, but I couldn't place it.

And then I remembered.

The night we got the call that Alexis was dead.

Last summer, Jason and Alexis took a well-deserved vacation to go hiking in the Rocky Mountains. He hadn't taken an extended break since he started the church more then ten years ago, and the church elders urged him to go. He didn't want to leave his congregation, but the elders assured him the church was in capable hands, and that everything would be in order when he got back. So, he scooped up Alexis and carried her off to the mountains for a month-long escape.

It only lasted a week.

Alexis suffered a terrible accident on the trip. They were hiking a steep slope covered in scree, and they both kept slipping on the loose rock. Jason had gotten nervous, he said, but thought they'd both be okay as soon as they got to the top of the ridge. He made it there first, but just a few feet from the top Alexis slipped again, this time sliding all the way down to the bottom of the slope.

Jason went down after her, screaming her name, but she didn't respond. When he got to her, she was unconscious and covered in blood. She was not just badly scraped up; she had hit her head. Hard.

Jason felt he had three choices. He could run back to

the campsite where he could get a cell signal to call emergency services, he could carry her back to the car and drive her to a hospital himself, or he could stay with her and pray. As much as he wanted to trust God in that moment, he said, he chose to run back to the campsite and call 911.

Alexis was transferred by helicopter to a hospital in Denver. Jason told them to spare no expense for her medical care, but she never regained consciousness. Her head wound was too severe, and the doctors pronounced her brain dead. Jason had no choice but to discontinue life support. She passed away peacefully afterward, in a matter of hours.

Only then did Jason call and tell us what happened. He had prayed that she would recover, so that he could have delivered news of a miracle rather than a tragedy. But "the Lord didn't see fit to heal her," he'd said. "In His perfect timing, he called her home."

He took the news with admirable serenity.

To Cameron and me, her death came as a complete shock. Alexis had been not just part of Jason's life, but of ours. We were going to miss her almost as much as Jason would.

I remembered that a sick feeling had settled over me then. A feeling of dreadful finality. Of permanence.

That same feeling was visiting me again.

I desperately wanted to sweep it away. If I could put the feeling out, as if it were garbage to be collected, it wouldn't be real. It wouldn't mean what it meant the last time. It wouldn't mean anything.

My thoughts drifted back to earlier that afternoon. The last time I saw Cameron.

We had pulled into the parking lot at Jason's church, probably around two o'clock. It took longer than it should have to get there, but it took longer than it should to get anywhere in L.A.

Before getting out of the car, Cameron had put his phone on airplane mode, as he always did when he was spending quality time with someone. That wasn't unusual for him. He liked to focus on the person was with, without being interrupted by phone calls and texts.

One thing did stand out to me about the church, though. It was the only thing that stood out about the whole day, actually.

The parking lot was empty. The church was huge, and it was always bustling with energy. They probably had about five thousand members and at least thirty staff. But that afternoon it was deserted.

I had remarked to Cameron that it was weird, but he remembered something about the staff being away on a prayer retreat for the week. Even though he wasn't worried, I waited to make sure he got inside before I drove away. It was a big expensive building, but it was in the middle of a bad neighborhood with a lot of gang activity. I wasn't going to leave him stranded outside if the doors were locked.

But the door opened. He turned and waved at me, and I drove home.

It never occurred to me that Cameron wouldn't be back with me that night.

I looked over at the dinner I had made for the two of us, cold and congealed on the kitchen table. My palms were sweating and my face was hot. The sick feeling hadn't gone away. I bustled about, scraping the food into containers and storing it in the fridge. I never let go of my phone, just in case.

Then the doorbell rang.

I looked at the clock.

It was eleven-thirty.

I could see red and blue lights flashing through the slits in the blinds.

I wanted to scream.

I knew what it meant.

Almost in a trance, I floated to the door and found my hand opening it.

It was a police officer. LAPD.

I nearly collapsed, but my legs held me up long enough to hear him say it.

Cameron was stabbed.

Hours ago.

In the church parking lot.

He was dead.

The Second Day

APRIL 5

3

I was pregnant.

The little white stick with the plus sign said so.

I was also about to be evicted.

The little white paper on my kitchen table said so.

It was more than two months since Cameron was killed, and I was barely able to function. I was supposed to play at a gig the week after he died. We both were, and I thought I could go and play without him. Do it for him, in a way, as a tribute or whatever. Stupid notion. I sobbed all the way to the studio in the car.

Before I could make myself go onto the recording stage, I spent so much time in the bathroom blowing my nose and wiping my eyes that I was seven minutes late. Under normal circumstances, that would be completely unacceptable. When I finally made my entrance, though, the entire orchestra stood up and applauded. For my bravery, I guess? At showing my face in public, while having a murdered husband?

It was all too much. I made it through the session, but I

was never able to go back again. I turned down so many gigs that I guess the contractor took me off the list, because I hadn't gotten a call in weeks. That would have been fine, except for the fact that my rent was overdue. And not only had I lost my husband, I'd lost both our income.

And if that drugstore pee stick was correct, I would soon be supporting a baby. A child. Cameron's child.

I was almost three months pregnant already. I was so overwhelmed with grief that I didn't even realize how long it had been since my last period.

My eyes burned with tears, as they almost always did. I'd given up make-up entirely. I indulged my sorrow for a good long while. And then I started to panic. What was I going to do?

I'd lost my career. There were a thousand piano players lined up to take my job, and I was certain one of them had done so by then. I'd probably never get my foot back in the door again. How could I play, anyway, with a baby to take care of?

The only saving grace I had since Cameron's murder was Jason. I never would have expected him to be such a strong presence, such a steadfast support. He was the only person I called after the LAPD Officer gave me the horrible news. Thank god I was finally able to reach him.

He drove to my apartment immediately, staying on the phone with me the entire time. He wouldn't let me hang up, because he didn't want me to be alone. Since he'd lost his own wife less than a year ago, he knew how devastating it was to lose a spouse.

In the aftermath, he simultaneously gave me all the space I needed to grieve and served as an ever-present comfort. He enlisted volunteers from his church to bring me food, so I wouldn't have to cook. As a result, I had the dubious privilege of sampling casserole recipes from seemingly every cuisine around the world.

He also acted as my liaison with the detectives on Cameron's case. No one knew exactly what happened, but as far as they could tell, Cameron was an innocent victim of gang violence. It turned out I should have listened to my intuition about the empty parking lot. The staff was indeed on a prayer retreat for the week, and the church was supposed to be closed. Jason was on the retreat, and had simply forgotten to text Cameron to cancel their lunch date.

The church had been broken into and vandalized during the week, which was why the door was unlocked when I dropped Cameron off. The police theorized that once Cameron found the church empty, he must have come back outside to look around. Then, while in the parking lot, some gang member stabbed him and robbed him, leaving him to bleed to death in the parking lot.

When he was found, his phone and the cash from his wallet were missing. At the time, the phone still hadn't been recovered. The police said they were looking for it, but they didn't believe it would provide anything that could help.

"What if there's something on it?" I asked the detective assigned to the case. "A photo, a video, a recording, anything? It could be the clue you need to find Cameron's killer."

"I take it you don't have the password to your husband's cloud account?" he had said.

"Of course I do. I've already logged in and checked it."

"And there are no photos or videos on the camera roll that could assist us?" He shuffled papers around, trying to brush me off.

"No, but—"

"We'll keep in touch with any developments, Ma'am."

He stood up and ushered me out of his office. I never got the chance to explain that Cameron always put his phone on airplane mode when he was out, so if by some chance he took a photo or video, it wouldn't have uploaded to the cloud yet. It would still be on his device unless and until the phone was reconnected to the internet.

If only I could have found that phone. But what was I going to do, drive my pregnant self down to South Central L.A. and start snooping around about a dead redhead? I wished I could. I thought about asking Jason to go with me.

I was being ridiculous.

He hid it well, but I was sure Jason was trying not to drown in his own guilt for forgetting to cancel the lunch with Cameron. I was certain he felt it was his fault that his brother was killed.

Of course, I was equally guilty for driving away and leaving him. Guiltier.

Maybe the only reason Jason was being so kind to me

was because he felt responsible for Cameron's death. Whatever his motivation, I was grateful. I needed help, and he was the only one who was offering it.

I looked around the apartment, wondering how I was going to keep it. I was five days late on that month's rent and my landlord had so kindly informed me that I had exactly three days to pay or get out. But I didn't have the money, which meant I was about to lose my home and everything in it.

Cameron and I had been scraping by as it was. We never had enough extra money to save up a decent emergency fund. What little we had was already used up. Our annual residual check was still months away, and I didn't think I could force myself to go back to work even if I did get a call.

I examined the pregnancy test one more time. The plus sign was starting to fade. I almost wanted that to mean that I wasn't really pregnant, that it was a mistake. I couldn't raise a baby alone.

But I didn't really want that. Because I realized, as tears stung my eyes yet again, this child would be all I had left of my Cameron.

Jason was due to be at my place any minute, so I wrapped the test in tissue and threw it away. I wasn't ready to share the news with anyone yet. Desperately, I scrubbed my face and wiped my eyes. It was no use. I looked like a mess all the time. But Jason had seen me at my worst, and he didn't care.

When I opened the door, Jason presented me with a bouquet of daffodils. I was a bit startled, as a man bringing flowers is usually a romantic gesture. But I knew that wasn't what it was.

"Rebirth and new beginnings," he said, handing me the yellow blooms. "The florist told me that's what they mean. It's too soon, I know. But the Lord heals."

I took the flowers and almost smiled. It was far too soon to talk of new beginnings. Cameron's clothes still had his smell. But daffodils had always been my favorite flower. I didn't think Jason knew that, but I couldn't resist their cheer, even then.

"Come in, Jason. No casserole?" I asked. I'd gotten used to seeing him with a glass-lidded ceramic dish wrapped in a handmade, quilted-fabric carrier supplied by the ladies of the church.

He winked at me as he came through the door. For a second, I paused, watching his back as he made his way to my kitchen. He'd never done that before.

I closed the door and joined him in the kitchen.

Since Cameron's death, Jason had gotten comfortable making himself at home in my apartment. He opened my fridge, took out a couple bottles of Mexican Coke, and popped the tops.

No alcohol for Jason.

"Sit down, Lara," he said. "There's something I want to talk to you about."

He pulled out a chair for me at my own dining table, and I sat. He put one of the Cokes in front of me, and took the seat across the table.

"Do you know the Bible story about the kinsman-redeemer?"

I wanted to scoff. Or snort, or laugh. Of course I didn't know the Bible story about the kinsman-whoever. I'd never been religious, and neither was Cameron. Neither was Jason, truth be told, until he decided to start a church. But whatever.

I just said, "No," and drank my Coke.

"It's not so much a story as a concept." He laid his hand gently on top of mine. The one not wrapped around the Coke, anyway. I looked down at it. What was going on?

"I know you're in trouble," he said. He was right, but how could he know that? I just found out I was pregnant an hour before. And I hadn't shared my money troubles with him, or anyone.

Tears blurred my eyes yet again. I tried not to blink so they wouldn't spill down my cheeks.

He went on, speaking in the softest, tenderest voice. His eyes so very, very gentle. Gratitude flooded my heart. I was so thankful for my brother-in-law.

"You've lost Cameron's income. And you're not working. You won't be able to keep this apartment unless you can pay for it."

I nodded. The tears spilled over.

"I want you to know you're not alone. With your permission, I'd like to act as your kinsman-redeemer."

I inhaled deeply. I still didn't know that was. It sounded… serious.

Jason saw my apprehension and squeezed my hand. He smiled, a sad, patronizing little smile.

I shifted in my seat. The situation had gotten weird and

uncomfortable really fast. I wished Cameron were there.

"In ancient times, when a family member was in trouble, it was the responsibility of the closest male relative to provide the help needed. His solemn duty, in fact. I recognize that you are incredibly vulnerable right now, Lara, and I am your closest male relative. If you'll permit me, I would like to make a proposal."

If I was prepared to be honest with myself, I would have said the conversation was bordering on creepy. Something in me wanted to run. But I withheld judgment until I found out what he was about to suggest. Besides, no one else was sitting across from me at my kitchen table, offering me a solution to my very dire problems.

"Propose, then," I said.

"Lara, will you walk with me in faith, as your husband?"

"What?" I yanked my hand away. I felt like I'd been slapped. That was absolutely not what I thought he meant.

He smiled.

Smirked.

No, he wouldn't smirk.

I was just in shock. Misinterpreting everything.

"Jason, is this some kind of joke? Don't do that. I can't even begin to laugh about this."

"No, Lara. I've prayed earnestly about this. Let me explain."

Jason stood up and led me to the couch in the living room. We sat next to each other. He leaned back into the cushions, but I perched on the edge, afraid to relax because I didn't know what was about to hit me.

"Lara, when I lost Alexis last year, it was the most difficult thing the Lord ever led me through. Of course I loved her, and I miss her, and I'm still grieving her. But worst of all has been the loss of companionship. She was my best friend. Someone to talk to about my day. Someone who saw me at my best, and at my worst, and still accepted me. Flaws and all."

He paused, checking to see if I was following him. I was.

"Once a man has been married, it's very hard for him to be unmarried. My bachelor days are behind me. Do you understand?"

I thought I did, but I didn't want to.

"Don't tell me you don't have women at the church throwing themselves at you," I said.

He waved his hand at me, fake modest. Obviously, I was right.

"My duty, as your kinsman, is to care for you. You're family. But I will admit I'm not entirely selfless here. As I said, I have needs, too. I was not kidding before, Lara. I would like to marry you—"

I opened my mouth to protest, because I couldn't possibly accept his awkward, abrupt offer, but he put his hand up to shush me. For some reason, I felt compelled to obey. My mouth snapped shut.

He continued.

"I would like to marry you, Lara. But please know that I don't expect you to love me. We will both know that this arrangement is one of me fulfilling my duty to care for you. You will move into my home with me, and I will take care of all your financial needs. You won't need to go back to work. There will always be a place for you to play piano at the church, if you like. When you're ready, of course. In return, I expect only friendship. The same as we have now. Maybe we'll grow to love each other one day, but we'll let time take care of that."

He smiled again. His eyes gentle that time. I scrutinized him, finding only fondness and sympathy. I didn't detect any ill intentions.

I'd always liked Jason. And Cameron loved him. Could we form a bond, over time? Forged by our mutual love of his brother, my husband?

I knew one thing. I would never get another offer like that.

I swallowed hard.

"Yes, Jason. I will marry you."

The Third Day

JUNE 15

4

Jason kept all the promises he made to me. We were married at his church, of course, but in the smallest possible ceremony. Nothing flashy, just the two of us, an Associate Pastor to officiate, and two witnesses. Our signatures on the marriage license, and the deed was done.

Getting married was a lot easier than moving out of my apartment. Jason paid an extra month's rent to give me time to move out. I had to go through all of Cameron's things. I wept over every dirty shirt, every unused razor, every crumpled sheet of music with his notations on it.

Jason helped me, coached me through it. He'd just been through a similar process after Alexis died, so he understood. He told me not to hang on to Cameron's stuff. That it wouldn't bring Cameron back, it would just prevent me from moving forward in life, from healing. Was he right? I didn't know.

But I got rid of almost everything. I even went through Cameron's trumpets. He had two B-flat trumpets, a C trumpet, a piccolo trumpet, a cornet, and a flugelhorn. Jason wanted me to sell them, but I couldn't imagine Cameron's cherished instruments going to strangers. Or worse, sitting in a pawn shop, unplayed. Instead, I gave them to one of Cameron's trumpet player friends who also taught private lessons. He said he had a few promising students who could use them.

But Cameron's Bach Strad B-flat… his most prized trumpet. The one he felt completely at one with. I could never part with that.

Music was his life. And his trumpet was part of him. I wished I could hear him play it one last time. He could sing through that trumpet. Wail through it, or scream. Sometimes even whisper. It was his voice. I missed it.

I kept it, safe in its case, under my bed. It was comforting. It made me feel Cameron was still with me.

Jason gave me my own room in his beautiful, enormous house, with an attached bathroom and a big king-sized bed of my own. We never discussed the sleeping arrangements before I moved in, and I didn't know what he would expect. But he never made me feel uncomfortable, or put me in an awkward position. I couldn't stand the thought of sleeping in the same room he and Alexis had shared not that long before, but I never had to say so.

He kept his room and gave me mine. My bed was big enough for two people, but he never tried to share it. We were friends. Companions. Just like he proposed.

But I had a secret.

My new husband still didn't know I was pregnant.

I was eating an enormous amount of food, trying to put on weight. It was working. I didn't look pregnant; I looked pudgy.

"Stress eating," I told Jason. "Should probably cut back."

He bought it.

But I couldn't go on that way any longer. My belly was starting to take on that telltale, rotund shape that betrayed the tiny human growing inside. And it was getting firm, even under the layer of flesh I'd put on.

There was no chance Jason would think it was his, because… well, we hadn't consummated our marriage. I didn't know how he would feel about raising his brother's child. I could only hope he'd love it like his own.

It was already late afternoon, so I puttered around in Jason's gourmet kitchen, trying to figure out what to make for dinner. I guessed it was my kitchen, too, but it still felt like I was a visitor in his house. Cameron and I used to come over, and I'd chat with Alexis while she cooked in that oven and set the table with those dishes. It was all very surreal.

And yet I was grateful.

Since I had a big surprise to spring on Jason, I decided to make a nice meal. Nice for me, anyway. I was a musician, not a chef. Since I married Jason, I tried to learn to cook, and I'd had a few minor disasters. I turned some really nice ribeyes into shoe leather once, and another time I served a chicken breast half raw in the middle. I was going to try to make up for the ribeyes that night.

I looked up some recipes online, gathered all my ingredients, and got started. It took me a couple of hours, but I finished the garlic mashed potatoes, gravy, and salad. I got the steaks in the oven, and they would be ready to be reverse-seared as soon as Jason walked in the door. I even had a cherry pie, although it was store-bought. I wasn't ambitious enough to try to make that one from scratch.

There was just enough time for me to change into a dress. Not a fancy one, just something a little nicer than the yoga pants I was wearing around the house all day. A quick brush through my hair and a little lipstick.

Jason's car pulled into the garage, and I started to sweat. I was nervous.

I still didn't know how to greet him when he came home from work. We didn't kiss, so I couldn't exactly greet him like a normal wife would. Most of the time I would stop whatever I was doing and go up to him and just say, "Welcome home." It was a little awkward.

In the last few weeks, though, we had started to hug each other. It was nice to have that touch, for both of us, I suspect.

That night I decided to wait for him in the kitchen. He came in through the garage, and when he didn't see me right away, he called, "Lara?"

"In the kitchen!"

He dropped his briefcase and found me. Was that a smile lighting up his face? For just a second? If I wasn't afraid of flattering myself, I might have thought he was starting to love me.

If I wasn't afraid of betraying Cameron, I might have thought I was starting to love him, too.

"Welcome home," I said. We embraced. It lasted a few seconds longer than usual. I closed my eyes, breathed him in, and it was over.

"You look beautiful," he said. I'm sure I blushed. "Whatever you made smells delicious. When do we eat?"

"Five minutes. Soon as I sear the steaks."

He disappeared to his home office to put away his briefcase. In a few minutes, he was back, ready for dinner. By some miracle, the steaks came out a perfect medium rare, and the potatoes had just the right amount of garlic. He entertained me with wild stories about a group of college students that started their summer internship at the church that week. The picture he painted of those sheltered kids from the Midwest trying to navigate South Central L.A. had me in fits. For a moment, I almost remembered what it felt like to be happy.

"You'd better get them a van or something," I told him between gasps. "Riding the city bus will get them killed!"

He winked at me across the table. That brought me up short. The winking still reminded me of Cameron.

But I had to let it go. Jason was my new husband, and I had an important family matter to discuss with him.

I took a breath, but before I had the chance to steer the conversation in the direction I wanted to, he asked, "Have you given any more thought to playing the piano at the church? Prayed about it?"

"Umm, not really. I don't know, Jason. I've just never been a church person, you know that."

"You'll get there."

I didn't know if I would, but I didn't say so.

I put down my fork and took a huge gulp of water.

"There's something else I need to tell you." I said. "It's important."

Jason put down his fork, too. He wiped his mouth with his napkin and took a drink. He studied me, waiting.

I cleared my throat.

"I'm pregnant."

Jason's eyes went wide. "But—"

"It's Cameron's."

"When?"

"What do you mean…?"

"When is the baby due?"

"Umm, October. Middle of October."

He pushed away from the table and stood up. I couldn't tell how he felt about it. He wasn't crying tears of joy, though, that much was obvious.

"That's only four months away. How long have you known?"

He didn't give me a chance to answer.

"You've kept this from me! Did you know before we got married?"

"Yes," I said. I looked down at the table, shame washing over me. Why did I feel so guilty?

"You're my wife." Jason's voice rose. "You should have told me!"

He grabbed his head with his hands and turned away from me. He uttered something under his breath, too low for me to hear, and went to the doorway. He paused, facing the wall. His hands slowly clenched. His right fist slammed into the wall, leaving a gaping, black hole.

I squealed in shock.

He spun around, fire in his eyes.

My hand flew to cover my mouth.

"Don't ever keep secrets from me again."

"I won't, Jason, I'm sorry."

"Swear it."

"I swear, Jason, I'll never keep secrets from you again."

He stalked out of the room, abandoning me to my shock and confusion. What just happened to the loving, selfless Jason I thought I knew?

So much for the idea of him being happy for me. For us.

I sat alone at the table for a few minutes, scared to make a move. Would he come back? Or should I chase after him? I didn't know, Cameron never stormed out on me like that. I didn't know what it meant.

Enough time went by that I figured he wasn't coming back. I decided to clean up the kitchen. Dinner was obviously over, so I might as well put things in order. Jason hadn't come out of his office, and I was scared to go up there. I'd never seen him in a rage.

Next thing I knew, I heard Jason's footsteps on the stairs. The front door opened, then slammed shut. I ran to the front window and peeked through the closed curtains. Jason was pounding his way down the sidewalk on foot, his hands jammed in his pockets. I guessed he just needed some air. Fine. Maybe he would cool off and we could talk about the baby when he got back. Like a normal married couple. Or at least like civil adults.

Behind me, in the sitting room, was the Steinway Baby Grand piano Jason bought for me as a wedding present. He had it delivered before I moved in. He said he wanted me to keep playing, even though I wasn't doing it professionally anymore. The gesture was thoughtful and touching. I loved the fact that he was trying to make me feel at home. I had cried out of both gratitude and guilt.

I didn't get him anything.

I'd told him that I practiced every afternoon while he was at the church. It was a lie. I hadn't been able to touch a piano since the last time I played at a recording session. It was too painful, because it reminded me of everything that Cameron and I shared.

But as I looked at that beautiful instrument, sitting alone in that big, expensive house… It seemed wrong not to play it. I ventured over, ran my fingers over the wood, and finally lifted the fallboard. I sat down. Touched the keys. Tested the action. My fingers knew just what to do. I played and played and played. Scales, arpeggios, etudes, classical, jazz, everything.

Before I knew it, two hours had passed. Jason wasn't back yet. I peeked through the curtains again, although it seemed foolish. Of course, he wasn't there. He'd be back when he was ready, I guessed.

Since it was late, I decided to get ready for bed. After washing my face and brushing my teeth, I rummaged through my pajama drawer. My eyes rested on a pretty silk nightgown I almost never wore. Something possessed me to change into it. What the hell, I thought, it was a hot night. Plus, I was about to grow way too big to fit into it again for a long, long time. I put it on, slipped between the sheets, and fell asleep.

I dreamed of Cameron. We were swimming together. I was drowning, but he saved me. I told him I had a secret. I was carrying his child, but I wasn't going to raise it with him, because I married his brother. He didn't get angry, or even sad. He winked at me and took me to bed. We snuggled together, just like we used to. He was so close, so warm. But something was wrong. Something was terribly wrong. What was it? What was wrong???

My eyes popped open. I gasped for breath.

"Cameron? Cameron!" His arms were tight around me. Squeezing me. I couldn't move. "Let me go!"

He did. I sat up in bed. Turned around.

Screamed.

It was Jason.

I forgot. Cameron was dead, and I forgot. How could I forget?

Jason sat up and wrapped his arms around me. "Shh…" he said. "Shh… it's okay. I'm your husband now."

But he was the wrong husband. "Why are you here? Why are you in my bed?" I sounded hysterical because I was.

I threw back the covers and discovered that Jason was naked. I hyperventilated. I liked Jason, I was grateful to Jason, and I married Jason. But I didn't want to sleep with Jason.

He stroked my hair, trying to calm me. "You look exquisite," he breathed into my ear. "Did you wear this for me?"

His hand traveled down my side, skimming over my body.

"It's time, Lara."

"For what?" My voice was weak and small.

His touch was tender, loving. He wasn't cruel or aggressive. He was lonely, and so was I. Why didn't I want it?

It wasn't our deal. But did I really expect that deal to last forever? He was a man, he had needs. I wasn't naïve. Deep down, I knew that becoming his wife would mean that eventually we would have to become one flesh.

I nodded my head and swallowed. With my consent, he peeled off my silk nightgown and laid on top of me. He consummated our union. I allowed it, but I didn't enjoy it.

He collapsed back against the sheets, panting and sweating.

I stared at the ceiling, feeling nothing.

"Say 'I love you,'" he said.

"Jason—"

"Say it, Lara. You're my wife, say it!"

"I need more time. I'm still…" I faltered.

He twisted the sheets in his fist. I heard him grind his teeth.

"'I. Love. You. Jason.' Say it."

"iloveyoujason."

He relaxed his grip and rubbed his knuckles. "Good," he said. We lay in silence for another minute or two, not touching.

Then he got out of bed and walked to the bathroom door. Before he went in, he turned to me.

"We're married now. No more playing brother-and-sister. Tomorrow you'll move into the master bedroom with me. And we'll tell the congregation the baby is mine. We'll say it was born premature."

He disappeared into the bathroom before I had a chance to say anything.

I swiped away the tears and pushed my fist into my mouth to keep from crying out. I could sleep with Jason, if that's what he wanted. I could even play piano at his stupid church if it would make him happy. But how could I ever deny that Cameron was the father of the miraculous child I was carrying?

Jason intruded on my thoughts by throwing open the bathroom door, a towel around his waist.

"I love you, Lara."

He was sincere. I wished he wasn't.

It would have been easier if he were a sadistic monster or an evil demon. But he wasn't. He was thoughtful, funny, charismatic, Cameron's-brother, Jason.

Wasn't he?

I didn't know what was going on with Jason, but for the first time I was afraid of him.

And I was afraid he really loved me.

The Fourth Day

SEPTEMBER 4

5

Church was just getting out. I was sitting in the front row of the enormous auditorium, having endured three (yes, three) services already that morning, during each of which Jason introduced me to his sizeable and enthusiastic congregation. Onstage.

Jason didn't warn me that he was going to call me up in front of everyone. Once he did, I basically had no choice but to come up on the platform and smile graciously. The lights were too bright for me to see the people in the congregation, but their applause was deafening. They were thrilled that Jason had a brand new wife and a baby on the way.

The place was nothing like I imagined church to be. Every time Jason had badgered me to play piano there, I pictured plunking out the accompaniment to "Holy, Holy, Holy" while a bunch of old folks sang out of tune. Turns out I couldn't have been more wrong. The church had a band, lighting, and a whole rock-concert vibe going. It was so loud, I don't even know whether the congregation was singing along or not.

Jason, though. Jason was on fire. When he gave his "talk" — apparently they didn't call it a sermon — he was more like a motivational speaker than an old-fashioned preacher. Of course, he pontificated about the whole kinsman-redeemer thing that morning, which made me blush up to my ears. It felt like everyone was staring at me.

Despite that, I had to admit he was very impressive. I was surprised how dynamic he was up there on that stage. I understood why so many people came to hear him every week. He was kind of a mini-celebrity.

Every Saturday night since we got married, Jason had asked me if I was ready to come to the church. Up until the night before, I'd said no. I didn't even know why. I guessed it was because I knew that once I did, our marriage would be very public. And that would mean it was all real.

But the baby was due in a month, and she was going to be very real. I couldn't keep pretending.

That wasn't the whole story, though. I was worried that the people at the church wouldn't like me. Wouldn't accept me as Jason's wife. They had loved Alexis and grieved with Jason when she died. It was over a year since then, but how would they feel knowing Jason remarried so quickly? Not to mention impregnated his new wife? At least that's what everybody believed.

Only he and I knew the truth.

I didn't want to keep that secret, but they were Jason's friends. Or fans, or whatever the church people are called. It wasn't my business to tell them the baby wasn't Jason's. They could believe whatever they want.

Cameron would have understood.

The band played as the people filed out of the aisles, exchanging fake smiles and gossiping loud enough to be heard over the music. I stood up to stretch my legs. My eight months pregnant body didn't like to sit for long periods of time. It didn't like to stand much, either. Walking was strenuous, too, which left lying down. I was looking forward to going home and doing just that. Jason was swarmed with people, though. Shaking his hand, hugging him, clapping him on the back. I didn't know how long it would be until we could leave.

I felt a tap on my shoulder, and I spun around, trying not to bump anyone with my belly. It was a man in a sport coat and slacks, probably around fifty years old. Gray hair and a mustache. And a subtle accent. German, maybe?

"You're Pastor Jason's wife?" he asked.

I nodded.

"Can we talk? Privately?"

I bit my lip. I didn't know the man. What could he want with me?

"It's about Cameron," he said. "Come with me."

My heart pounded. I hadn't heard Cameron's name spoken by anyone for months. Even Jason had stopped talking about him. Whoever the stranger was, if he had information about my Cameron, I needed to know.

The man took hold of my elbow and steered me out of the auditorium, into a small room with a fake fireplace and fake plants. He closed the door behind us. It was empty in there, and quiet.

He gestured toward the sofa, offering me a seat. I took it. He sat opposite me in an upholstered wing-backed chair.

"I'm on the Security Team here at the church," he said. "But I'm also a detective. I'm not officially assigned to Cameron's case, but since he was Pastor Jason's brother, I've been following it."

"Yes?"

I was breathless. For the last seven-and-a-half months, there were no updates on the case. I'd called the police every week, badgering them about finding Cameron's killer. But all they would tell me is that they'd found no witnesses, and they hadn't recovered his phone. Without those, there was no hope of identifying the murderer.

Maybe the man knew something more.

He leaned forward in his chair, squinted his eyes, and said, "It's time to drop it. The police have."

"What do you mean?" Tears pricked my eyes again. "They're still investigating!"

The man stood up and advanced on me. I was glued to the sofa, and he towered over me. He was between me and the door. I felt trapped. I wanted to escape, but something told me he wouldn't let me if I tried.

"They can't officially close the case yet, but it's over. They've dropped it, and you should, too."

I fought back the wail that wanted to escape from the depths of my gut. "No!"

He stuck his index finger in my face.

"Stop looking for that phone. For Jason's sake."

And he strode out of the room.

I felt my jaw clench, and my eyebrows knit together in a scowl. The way he said that, commanded it, riled me. What right did he, or anyone, have to tell me to forget about finding my husband's killer?

Up until that moment, I'd done nothing but trust the police to find him. But that had produced exactly zero results.

Something about that man's threatening demeanor rankled me. It took a lot of gall to corner a grieving, pregnant widow and warn her to back off the L.A. Police Department. That told me there was more to the crime than I could have guessed.

I took a deep breath, pushed back my hair, and blew out a puff of air. I had some serious thinking to do.

Before I got a chance, a petite, curly-haired woman cracked the door open and poked her head in.

"Lara, right?" she asked.

"Yes."

She slipped into the room, shut the door behind her, and locked it.

"I'm so glad you finally came to church this morning. Girl, what took you so long?"

The answer to that question would have been very complicated. I didn't know what to say, so I said nothing.

"Doesn't matter," she said, taking a seat on the sofa next to me. "Listen, I'm Maxine. Alexis was my best friend."

"She never mentioned you," I said. To be honest, I kind of thought Alexis didn't have time for any close friends.

"I know, she wouldn't have. She didn't want Jason to know about our friendship. He would have told her not to contact me. We only have a minute, so please let me get this out, okay?"

She seemed earnest, sincere. I let her continue, even though I already had so many questions.

"Jason is not what he seems. Maybe you've figured that out. Am I telling you something you already know? Whatever. This is important. He was controlling, like super controlling, of Alexis. He wouldn't let her go anywhere or see anyone without his permission. And he berated her all the time, yelling at her about how stupid she was and how lucky she was to have him. How she could never leave him because no one else would ever put up with her, that kind of stuff."

Maxine looked me deep in the eye. Her gaze felt like it penetrated down to my soul.

"She thought she could appease him, and Lord knows she tried. It started with just yelling, but eventually he got violent. He started to hit her, throw her around. He was careful to keep the bruises where they would be covered by her clothes, but she showed them to me. She thought she could live with it. But you know what happened?"

I realized I was shaking. Shudders ran through my body, and I couldn't control them.

"She got pregnant," said Maxine. "She called me when Jason was at work. I told her I would come pick her up from the house right then and get her out. But you know what?"

I shook my head. I had an awful feeling I knew what was coming.

"She wouldn't let me. She still loved Jason, she said. Just this one last trip to the mountains, she said, then she would leave. I begged her not to go. But she did. And we both know what happened, don't we?"

"We do," I whispered.

"Does this ring any bells with you?"

I thought about Jason's reaction when I told him I was pregnant.

"Yes," I whispered again.

"You've got to get out," said Maxine. "Please don't make the same mistake as Alexis. Please."

She pressed a piece of paper into my hand.

"It's my phone number. Please, please call me as soon as you're ready to leave. Anytime, day or night."

I opened my mouth to tell her all the reasons I couldn't leave Jason. How he'd been so good to me, how he was an old friend, how he was the only thing I had left of my real husband, Cameron.

Before I could say any of those things, the doorknob jiggled. Someone was trying to get in, but it was locked.

"Lara? Lara, darling, you in there?"

It was Jason.

Maxine put a finger to her lips to shush me. She tiptoed over to the coat closet, eased open the door, and snuck inside.

I got up off the sofa, rumpled my hair, and kicked off my shoes before going to the door.

"Jason!" I yawned and rubbed my eyes. "I'm so sorry. I was exhausted. I needed to grab a little nap, but I didn't want to interrupt you when you were talking with everyone."

I gave him a peck on the cheek.

"Thanks for coming to find me."

I collected my shoes, hoping to scoot out before he had a chance to discover Maxine in the closet. We did.

The rest of the day passed uneventfully, except for the fact that I couldn't stop thinking about everything Maxine had said. It was true that Jason was harboring a rage inside of him, but most of the time he kept it under control. Could he really have been violent with Alexis? Maybe even… caused her death?

The thought was too frightening, so I pushed it away. He was all I had.

When we laid down together in bed, Jason held me like he did every night since I started sharing his bed. He fell asleep in minutes, but I lay awake, replaying all the times Cameron and I spent with Jason and Alexis. Had I ever seen warning signs? I couldn't think of any. He was always so charming, so generous. A great guy.

I sank into a dreamless sleep. I didn't know how long it lasted, but something caused me to stir. My eyes were closed, but I was aware that Jason was no longer in bed with me. I heard voices, faint voices, drifting down the hallway.

I sat up. Why was the bedroom door open? Where

was Jason?

I strained to hear the voices. There were two. Male. One was Jason, and the other…

Cameron.

All drowsiness instantly dissolved. I was wide awake then. Straining, straining to hear.

I couldn't understand the words, but from the tone, it sounded like Cameron and Jason were arguing. They were agitated, tense. Angry. Until…

A loud grunt. A painful one.

Scuffling.

Groaning.

Jason's voice again.

And…

Silence.

Awful silence.

Softly, a drawer opened and shut. I barely heard it, but it was there.

A door closed down the hallway. Jason's office.

I slid back down under the covers, closed my eyes, facing the wall. Deep breaths, slow breaths, pretend-sleep breaths.

Jason closed the bedroom door and climbed into bed beside me.

I didn't sleep the rest of the night.

In the morning, I made my husband an extra-nice breakfast of sausage, eggs, and toast. I couldn't wait for him to leave. I was so eager, I overdid it with the helping. I ironed his shirt, filled his travel mug with coffee, and offered to grab his briefcase from his office.

"No! No, no, no, you've outdone yourself this morning, Lara." He rubbed my bulging belly. "You need to rest. Take care of yourself and our child."

He ran upstairs to fetch his briefcase, then kissed me as I twisted the baby inside me away from him.

Finally, he was in the car, out of the garage, and down the street.

Though it killed me, I waited another ten minutes until I was certain he wasn't coming back. He should be on the freeway by then, past the point of no return. I should be safe until evening.

My heart raced. My intuition told me not to do what I was about to do. Something inside me knew I was about to blow up the life I'd created from the shattered pieces Cameron left behind. To destroy the stable environment my baby could be born into.

But I needed the truth.

Everything depended upon it.

So I climbed the stairs, trembling. Down the hall, past the bedroom, to Jason's office. The doorknob slipped in my sweating palm, but it was unlocked. I twisted the knob and pushed.

I'd never set foot in Jason's home office before. He hadn't said it was off-limits, but he'd never invited me inside. Since he so generously took me in when I was desperate, I'd always been as respectful as possible of his private space. I'd never even been to the church until yesterday, so I had no business in there, anyway.

Until that morning.

I knew he wasn't there, but I looked over my shoulder anyway.

I was alone.

The desk was in the corner of the office, facing the window. I sat in Jason's luxurious leather chair. The view from that seat was the best in the house, but I didn't care. I was on a mission.

I opened the top drawer of the desk and looked inside. Neat and tidy. Pens, pencils, paper clips, each in their own little organizer. Probably Alexis's doing.

There were three drawers on the side of the desk. The top one held a couple of phone chargers, note paper, some scissors, and a stapler. The next one was just stationery with Jason's name on the church letterhead and matching envelopes. The bottom drawer held hanging files.

I sat back in the chair, replaying the sound I heard last night, just before the office door closed. It was a desk drawer, I knew it. What did I miss?

Being ever so careful not to disturb the organization of the drawers, I searched them all again. That time I rifled through the note papers in the top drawer, and the files in the bottom one.

Inside a file folder, I felt something. I grabbed for it.

My hand closed on a small rectangular device. I pulled it out of the drawer and looked.

I almost choked.

It was what I wanted. I just never thought I'd find it in Jason's office.

Cameron's phone.

There was no mistaking it. It had the treble clef cover I bought him for his birthday. And the crack in the screen from when he dropped it in the studio parking garage.

If Jason had Cameron's phone…

If he'd had it that whole time…

I couldn't form the sentence, even in my own mind.

Not yet.

My hands trembled as I powered the phone on.

Time stood still as I waited for the screen to light up with Cameron's wallpaper and icons.

I was afraid of what I was about to find.

There was one thing I had to check first.

I swiped up.

I was right. The phone was still on airplane mode. Cameron must have put it on and never had the chance to go back online.

My eyes teared up again, thinking about Cameron's last moments.

I could hardly believe what it meant.

If I wasn't hallucinating last night… If I really did hear Cameron's and Jason's voices… Then this phone contains a recording of the two of them having an argument. Just before he died.

Hesitating, blinking back tears, my trembling finger tapped the photo app. Instantly, a video started to play. A video I'd never seen before.

I forced myself to watch it through.

The tears wouldn't stop then. They wrenched through me, progressing to racking sobs.

But I could be strong. I had to be strong for my child. Cameron's child.

I connected the phone to the internet. As soon as the video synced to Cameron's cloud account, I put it back on airplane mode, replaced it in the file folder, and left the office as I found it.

Then I called Maxine.

The Fifth Day

OCTOBER 3

6

Only one thing mattered on that day.

My beautiful daughter finally arrived, safe in my arms. She was tiny. And perfect. And she had Cameron's red hair.

How he would have adored her.

I would never forgive Jason for taking him away from me. From us.

I only watched the video on Cameron's phone one time. That's all I could handle. But it was clear enough what had happened.

It had been a month since I called Maxine that afternoon. Without hesitation, she'd come to the house and gotten me. She swooped in, helped me pack up some clothes, and took me to her place while Jason was at the church. She warned me I may never see the inside of Jason's house again, so I made sure to take Cameron's Bach Strad. My most precious possession.

Since I had access to the video through Cameron's cloud account, I showed it to her. I had to leave the room because I couldn't stand to hear Cameron's horrible groans again, the last sounds he made before he died. The thought of it made me want to vomit.

She went over it several times, though, and gave me her assessment. Since there was no image at the beginning of the video, just black, she assumed the phone was in Cameron's pocket. Underneath a lot of rustling noise, she heard the two male voices, agitated and arguing.

"You're not fooling anyone. I know what you're doing," said the first voice, which I know for a fact was Cameron.

The second, muffled voice said, "I'm only trying to bring us closer as a fam—"

"I'm telling you to leave her the hell alone!" Cameron exploded with once-in-a-lifetime level force.

Immediately after that came Cameron's horrible grunt, a sickening thud, and the phone tumbling onto the ground.

Up until that point, Maxine said it was unclear whether the second voice belonged to Jason or not. But when the phone fell, the camera landed face up and it captured a clear shot of Jason's face when he picked up the phone. Just before he stopped the recording.

Maxine was convinced it was more than enough evidence to take to the police. Especially since Cameron's phone was still sitting in Jason's desk drawer. I was skeptical, because of the detective who had confronted me at the church. He told me to drop it, that the case was basically closed.

"Who was this guy?" Maxine had asked. "Describe him to me."

I told her about his gray hair and mustache, and the accent.

"Girl, that is no detective. That's Karl, the Executive Pastor at the church. And Jason's personal yes-man."

"What?"

"He just wanted you to back off. I bet Jason put him up to it."

That was all I needed. The idea that Jason would sic his lackeys onto me, to prevent me from finding out he killed my husband… It lit a fire under me.

"Let's go to the police. Right now," I told Maxine.

She drove me to the LAPD station, and we met with the actual police detective I'd been harassing on the phone for so many months. He was loath to see me until I showed him the video. For the first time, I felt he was taking the case seriously.

"Where is Cameron's phone now?" he asked, when I told him how I got the video.

"Still in Jason's desk drawer. In his home office."

The detective practically jumped out of his chair, saying he needed to get a search warrant, pronto. Maxine and I waited while he got on the phone with a judge. He had the warrant within an hour, but it looked like Jason was going to get home from work before the police would get there to perform the search.

They didn't want to give him any chance to be suspicious, in case he would try to dispose of the evidence. So I had to stall him to keep him from coming home.

I called Jason and asked if we could meet at a

restaurant for dinner. I pretended I'd been missing him all day and wanted to spend a nice evening with him, since the baby was coming so soon. Smiling through that dinner with him was the hardest thing I'd ever done.

But it worked.

The police found the phone in his desk drawer. They turned the house upside down, looking for anything else they might find, including anything that could implicate him in Alexis's death. No one would tell me whether they found any such evidence or not.

But the phone itself was enough to arrest Jason on suspicion of Cameron's murder.

At the arraignment, the judge granted bail. Of course, he had plenty of money to pay it, so he was out after only twenty-four hours.

Maxine told me he was back in the pulpit Sunday morning, urging the church to pray for his wayward wife, who was making false accusations against him. He never missed a service, and the church seemed like they were bound and determined to stand by their man.

I knew he would ask them to help pay his legal bills, and they probably would. He would get the best defense attorney money can buy.

I hoped the justice system would do its job anyway. If so, he'd be convicted of Cameron's murder and thrown in prison for the rest of his natural life.

If not, he'd go on raking in tons of money and lying to people about who he truly is.

But on that day, that glorious, perfect day, the only thing that mattered to me was that I was holding my newborn daughter. Camille. She was healthy and we were both safe.

I would figure the rest out later.

Cameron would be proud.

...Love, Mother

7

Dear Camille,

After everything I've told you, I wish I could finish with a happy ending. But it wasn't meant to be.

The charges against Jason were dropped. It made no sense when it happened, and it still doesn't. I can only speculate, but he has made himself into a powerful and influential man with an extensive network of connections. I assume he called in a favor with someone in a position to grant it.

Whatever took place behind closed doors, he will never be convicted of murdering my husband. Your father.

Yes, that's right. My Cameron, my beloved Cameron, is your true father.

When I was pregnant, Jason told the church that you were our child. The congregation was thrilled. I should have contradicted him. Set the record straight right then. But I didn't, and now everyone believes that you are Jason's.

You probably believe it yourself. You will have heard it

your entire, comfortable life. The daughter of a celebrity L.A. pastor.

But it's not true; I have the documents to prove it. I had the hospital perform a paternity test before you and I were discharged. I will keep it stored away, safe until you are ready to read this.

If I've done my duty as a mother, you will love Jason. He will be the only daddy you've ever known. For that reason, you may never accept that he could be a murderer.

Ask him.

I did, after the prosecutor dropped the case against him. He confessed to me that he killed his own brother, the only man I ever loved.

And Alexis? He killed her, too. His own wife.

He admitted everything to me. He seemed proud of himself.

But why? Why would he do these terrible things when he already had a lovely wife, a beautiful home, and a wildly successful career?

Because he wanted me, he says. Sometimes, when I'm feeling brave, I let myself wonder why. I never come up with a reason. I'm not that special.

Maybe he was jealous of Cameron.

Maybe he wanted the one woman he couldn't have.

Or maybe obsession just isn't logical.

I don't love Jason. But he does love me, in his own twisted way. He thinks I belong to him, and I suppose now I do.

So you see, my child, I can never leave him. If I did, I'm afraid he would kill me, too. And the one thing I cannot do is abandon you.

I will do whatever it takes to keep you safe. I will serve Jason, I will honor Jason, and I will praise Jason. In private and in public. And I will smile through the whole thing.

He's gotten everything he wanted. I only hope he doesn't get you, too.

With all my love,
Mother

THE END

Things couldn't possibly be worse.

Or so William Cox believes.

When a cruel tragedy tears his family apart, he has no choice but to beg a shady family friend for help.

He gets what he needs, but at a terrible price.

Against his will, he becomes embroiled in a vile illegal scheme. Trapped by the crimes he's forced to commit, he can't go back to his life without implicating himself.

Will he end the corruption, even if it means endangering the lives of his entire family?

Or… with his newfound status and wealth…
does he even really want to?

<u>ALTERED WILL</u>

A surprising new psychological thriller from

Holly Sheidenberger

A prequel to Related By Blood

COMING SOON

**How far would you go to protect your child
from danger?**

Maren is too busy to think about it.

She's eight months pregnant, consumed with
designing her latest fashion line, and desperate for the
approval of the one woman who won't give it—
her mother.

But when Dorla—a troubled client with a delusional
mission—insinuates herself deep into Maren's life,
Maren's carefully curated world begins to unravel.

Soon she finds herself and her unborn baby
ensnared in a trap she can't escape.

As Dorla's dark obsession spirals toward a horrifying
climax, Maren faces the unthinkable.

Can she protect her baby from a terrible fate?

Or is she already too late?

<u>THE SANGUINE SCISSORS</u>

A chilling new psychological thriller from

Holly Sheidenberger

COMING SOON

She wants her life back…
How far will she go to get it?

Fifteen years ago, Cleo was entangled with Harris—
the son of a powerful U.S. senator—
when everything went wrong.

One impulsive moment.

One tragic accident.

One cover-up that cost her everything she loved.

Now, she's kept her silence. She's played by their
rules. But the life she lost still haunts her,
and she's done waiting.

What begins as a bold move to reclaim her future
quickly spirals into obsession, manipulation,
and dangerous delusion.

As secrets are uncovered and loyalties shift, Cleo's
carefully constructed world begins to crack.

How far would you go to rewrite your past?

<u>RELATED BY BLOOD</u>

A razor-sharp psychological thriller novel from

Holly Sheidenberger

AVAILABLE NOW

ABOUT THE AUTHOR

Holly Sheidenberger is a psychological thriller author whose work has been described as "gritty," "addictive," and filled with "jaw-dropping revelations around every corner."

Before turning to writing, she worked as a stage actress, where she developed a fascination with complicated roles and the dark intricacies of human behavior.

She brings that experience to her stories, which are fueled by an insatiable curiosity about why people do what they do.

With roots in misty Seattle and sunny Los Angeles, she now writes from the Sonoran Desert of Arizona.

In a home filled with music and story, she shares her life with her husband, Hollywood composer and musician Todd Sheidenberger, and their four daughters.